THE SLIME WAS HUNTING FOR MEAT . . .

From the depths of the pond the slime, now as big as a house, reared up like a huge, stench-filled Loch Ness monster. The whole golf course was shaking as if an earthquake had hit. It was unbelievable. Across the course people stopped playing and just leaned on their clubs and stared.

A hawk dove low over the water, and suddenly the slime began to tremble violently. Pieces of garbage that it had picked up at the dump were shaking loose and splashing into the water. Then, while everyone watched in horror, the slime reared up again. It stretched out a long slimy arm and shot upward, grabbing the squawking hawk and sucking it back inside the mound of goop.

Read these other **BONE CHILLERS** from
HarperPaperbacks:

*coming soon

BONE CHILLERS

SLIME TIME

BETSY HAYNES

HarperPaperbacks
A Division of HarperCollins*Publishers*

This is a work of fiction. The characters, incidents, and dialogues are products of the author's imagination and are not to be construed as real. Any resemblance to actual events or persons, living or dead, is entirely coincidental.

HarperPaperbacks *A Division of* HarperCollins*Publishers*
10 East 53rd Street, New York, N.Y. 10022

Copyright © 1996 by Betsy Haynes and
Daniel Weiss Associates, Inc.

Cover art copyright © 1996 Daniel Weiss Associates, Inc.

First printing: May 1996

Printed in the United States of America

HarperPaperbacks and colophon are trademarks of HarperCollins*Publishers*

❖ 10 9 8 7 6 5 4 3 2 1

For Alex Smith and his friend Jesse,
in Roselle Park, New Jersey

Chapter

It was just a cold at first and a terrible runny nose. My nostrils were getting all sore and red, and I felt as if the end of my nose would fall off if I rubbed a tissue against it one more time. I went into the bathroom and looked through the medicine cabinet. There were three old bottles of cold medicine.

I knew that I was supposed to take two tablets, but there was only one pill in each bottle. That's something my dad always does—he buys new stuff before we finish the old stuff. He also puts empty orange juice cartons back in the refrigerator. It drives my mom crazy.

As I was looking at the bottles, trying to decide which pills would work best, I could feel a warm dribble of snot sliding down my upper lip, heading straight for my mouth. Quickly I tore some toilet paper off the roll and pressed it against my nose. It felt as if I was rubbing salt into an open wound, and I leaned against the sink in shock.

I should never have ignored the warning on the label. You know, the one that says not to take more than one drug at a time without a doctor's supervision. If only I could have known in advance what misery I was about to bring to my entire town. Snodgrass, which until then had been a normal, peaceful place to live, would never be the same again.

But I was desperate. My nose hurt and I felt like a snotty disaster area. To top it all off, I knew that if I missed soccer practice again, Coach Powers would kick me off the team.

Since the pills were old, I figured they were probably pretty weak. So I popped all three into my mouth, one from each bottle, and then I downed them with a gulp of water.

My body felt tingly and my nostrils began to twitch. I sneezed. The inside of my throat was hot.

How long will it take before they start to work? I wondered.

"Achoo!"

I was in the hot-lunch line at school. The good news was that my nose had stopped running. The bad news was that I was sneezing uncontrollably.

"Jeez, Jeremy Wilson! You just sneezed all over me!" My best friend, Luke Damato, was wrinkling his nose at me and wiping off his face with his hands. "Yuck! It's disgusting!" His pale face was flushed with anger.

My sneeze had hit him like the blast from a fire hose.

"I didn't mean to," I said lamely. "It just happened. Honest."

"Yeah? Well, cover your mouth when you sneeze. Didn't your parents teach you anything? I don't want your stupid germs. Got it?"

"Okay, okay," I said. I didn't want my best friend mad at me.

A second later I sneezed again. All over Luke. Only this time I didn't even feel it coming on, so I couldn't cover my mouth.

I stood there helplessly, watching the droplets of snot bead up on Luke's face like rainwater on the hood of my dad's car.

Luke started ranting and raving again.

"Jeremy, you bonehead! Do you want me to get sick?"

I riveted my eyes to the floor, trying to think of some way to explain that I couldn't *help* sneezing! The medicine was making me feel weird—dizzy and lightheaded.

Suddenly I noticed that little drops of snot

were rolling across the floor toward each other. They stuck together and formed one big slimy green ball, about the size of a baseball.

I'm seeing things, I thought. *I must be really out of it.*

I started to point the slime out to Luke, but he was too busy yelling at me. His face was purple.

"I told you I didn't want your germs! That's what I'm going to call you from now on: Germ. Instead of Jeremy Wilson you're Germ Wilson. *Germ! Germ! Germ!* Get it?"

But I didn't look up. I was still staring at the glob of slime on the floor. It was growing. At least I thought it was. Or could it be my imagination?

The green ball jiggled slightly, sort of like the shimmy of a spoonful of gelatin. And when it jiggled, I swear it got bigger. My heart jumped into my mouth. I blinked and looked again. How could I be sure?

I looked frantically up the hot-lunch line. The line was creeping toward the steam tables. I spotted the paper-napkin box and grabbed a handful of napkins. Then I scooped up the slime and stuffed it into the pocket of my jeans.

Chapter 2

uke hadn't seen me stick the slime ball in my pocket. The line had finally gotten to the steam tables, and he wiped his hands down the legs of his jeans and grabbed a tray. I grabbed one, too.

"You know you've wrecked my appetite?" he grumbled out of the side of his mouth.

I shrugged. My stomach felt like a lump of heavy stone. *Something is going very, very wrong,* I thought.

Luke skipped the chicken nuggets, the whipped potatoes, and the creamed corn.

He sailed on past the tuna casserole and those hard brown things the school passed off as hamburgers. I knew where he was going.

It was the same place he always went when he said he wasn't hungry—the desserts. That was probably why he weighed almost twice as much as I did. He was also much taller than me, and with his bright red hair he always stood out in a crowd. Coach Powers said that he would make a great goalie if he practiced really hard. But Luke liked to do his own thing. He never followed instructions—not even the coach's.

I always had fun hanging out with Luke, but sometimes he could get me in trouble. If he hadn't persuaded me to skip all those practices so that we could play Mad Dog at the arcade or get hot-fudge sundaes at Bernie's, I wouldn't be in the trouble I was in with the coach.

Luke plunked a dish of chocolate pudding topped with fake whipped cream, a piece of dry-looking yellow cake with white icing, and a slice of cherry pie onto his tray and scooted toward the cashier.

I grabbed a hamburger and a carton of milk, but I still felt too nervous to eat. *There's no way I saw what I think I saw,* I reminded myself as I sat down.

Suddenly the slime ball slid out of my pocket onto the bench beside me. Had it moved by itself? It looked lumpy—almost pimply—and was covered with a damp, bright green sheen. I threw a paper napkin over it and glanced across the table at Luke to see if he'd noticed. He hadn't. He was too busy scraping the last of the warm, gooey chocolate pudding out of his dish.

All around us kids were pushing and shoving their way to tables. They were whizzing straw wrappers at each other and stealing each other's french fries. It was just an ordinary lunch period. For everybody but me!

I took a bite of my hamburger and tried to act normal. But as I chewed the meat a vision of the chunky slime ball rose vividly before me. I started to gag, and I spit my food back onto my plate.

Luke was working on his cake, and he didn't talk or look up as he shoveled in his food.

I couldn't help but glance down at the place on the bench where the slime was sitting. And in that moment everything changed for me. The slime stretched itself out, long and narrow like an elephant's snout. Then it oozed its way out from under the napkin and snatched at some hamburger meat that had fallen off my plate. It sucked it up and jerked back under the napkin!

I thought for a moment of the warning labels that I had so foolishly ignored this morning. What if something horrible had happened when I mixed the different cold medicines? What had I created?

The slime was wiggling around under the napkin like it was trying to get more comfortable and couldn't.

Then I heard the napkin tearing. And saw the glob of slime, with bits of paper napkin stuck all over its surface, jolt across the bench. It was moving and it was growing. Any second it would be so big that Luke would see it over the table. And if Luke could see it, so could all the other kids in the cafeteria.

I had to do something. And there was only one thing that made any sense. I had to get rid of it!

I grabbed the slime with both hands and clutched the gooey mass tightly under my shirt. Then I jumped up and ran out of the cafeteria as fast as I could.

I rocketed through the swinging doors and into the hall, not knowing which way to go. I was getting more nervous by the minute.

Only a few kids were in the halls. Most were still eating lunch. I took off at a trot for the boys' bathroom. There was a big trash can in there. I'd chuck the slime ball into the trash and be rid of it. Then the janitor would empty the trash into the Dumpster behind the school after classes let out for the day and the garbage truck would take the slime to the dump, where it would be buried under tons of junk.

And I would never ever have to see it again.

Chapter

"**H**ey, Germ, where'd you go in such a hurry?" Luke called out.

I was standing outside the boys' bathroom. I had just dumped the slime ball into the trash.

"What do you mean?" I asked, faking innocence.

"You know what I mean," Luke said, and scowled at me. "In the cafeteria just now. You didn't even take your stuff to the tray return."

"When you gotta go . . ." I said, shrugging and grinning sheepishly.

Luke didn't look convinced, but he didn't argue, either. "At least you aren't sneezing anymore," he admitted.

I hadn't thought about that. The idea made me feel better. No more sneezes meant no more slime balls.

"Come on," Luke continued. "Some of the guys are shooting hoops out on the playground." He started moving down the hall toward the door.

My feet wanted to go with him, but my brain told them to stay right where they were. A kid was going into the bathroom. I had to stay and see what happened.

"Um . . . can't," I said lamely.

Luke put his hands on his hips and looked at me as if I'd gone crazy. "Why not?"

Another kid shoved open the bathroom door and went inside. I held my breath.

Luke was glaring at me and tapping his foot impatiently. "You're acting really strange today," he said. "Do you want to tell me what's going on?"

"It's—it's nothing," I stammered. "I just

don't feel that well." *And then, of course, there's the fact that I've sneezed out some sort of creature from the green lagoon.*

Then I nodded toward the rest-room door and shrugged. "When you gotta go . . ." I added.

Luke shook his head in exasperation. "Jeez! Hurry, okay?"

I nodded and he walked down the hall, shaking his head and muttering.

As soon as he was out of sight I hurried into the bathroom. I almost ran into the first kid on his way out. He looked okay. I mean, he wasn't freaking or anything.

A fifth grader named Trevor was still in the bathroom. Since he was a year behind me, I didn't know him very well. He was hunched over the trash can with his left foot on the rim, tying his sneaker. He had the whole trash can leaning on a slant, and a few of the paper towels on the top were sliding out.

Then one of them moved all by itself in a little bumpy, burping motion. A piercing odor filled the air, like a mixture of gourmet cheese and old rotting flowers.

But Trevor just kept on fooling with the laces on his sneaker. It was taking him forever to finish tying them!

Suddenly a disgusted look crossed his face and he started sniffing suspiciously in my direction.

"That is foul!" he said.

"He who smelt it, dealt it," I said, trying to buy time. Maybe I could distract him so that he wouldn't start to wonder why I was just standing there watching him.

He didn't say anything. Maybe he was scared of me because I was a year older. Maybe he was just overcome by the stench.

He quickly turned toward the door to leave, but as he lifted his foot and let the trash can slide back into place a lump of green bulged up through the paper towels.

Chapter

I sucked in my breath. It looked like somebody was hiding underneath the soggy paper towels and blowing a huge bubble out of green bubble gum.

Did Trevor have his eyes closed? How could he help but see it?

I thought maybe I should just get out of there while I could. Even if Trevor had seen the slime, he'd have no way of knowing that it had anything to do with me. My secret would still be safe. *Just stay cool,* I told myself as I took in a quick, sharp breath.

I turned to dash out, but the door banged open and Luke barged into the bathroom.

"Come on, Germ. What's taking you so long? We need one more player."

Trevor glanced over at Luke and then headed out the door without a word. Had he seen anything?

"Did you hear me? I—" Luke stopped in midsentence, and his chin dropped so far it almost bumped his chest. He was looking straight at the slime ball. "What the . . . "

I didn't know what to say. My mind was racing, trying to think of a way to explain to Luke what had happened.

Luke snapped his mouth shut. He began to creep slowly toward the trash can as if he were sneaking up on his own shadow. The slime oozed over the edges of the trash can, covering it completely like a lid. It made a wet hissing noise, almost as if it were sighing. It had definitely grown!

Luke stood still for a moment, staring at the lumpy mass. Then he turned to me. His green eyes were wide and gleaming. He looked like a mad scientist. Anyone meeting the two of us now would assume that he had made the slime and that I was an innocent bystander. But this time I was the guilty one.

I knew there wasn't any use lying anymore, so I told him what I knew.

"You mean it's snot!" he bellowed. "How did it get so big? I thought you quit sneezing."

"I did," I said weakly. "It's . . . it's *growing*."

Luke staggered backward, like I'd just hit him with a two-ton snowball. Then he sort of recovered and gave me a sarcastic look. "Riiiiight."

"Something terrible is happening," I said. "It's like a nightmare, and I don't know how to stop it!" I was talking so fast even I couldn't keep up with what I was saying. "I'll die if anybody finds out I sneezed up that thing. That's why I brought it in here. I have to hide it. But now—" I didn't know what to say or what to do. I just looked helplessly at Luke, pleading with my eyes. "What am I gonna do?"

Luke shook his head in amazement. "I'm sure we can work out a simple solution," he said. He shot a quick look at the trash can and turned away quickly. "Let's try and retrace exactly what happened. When did it first begin growing?"

"I don't know," I said. "I never thought it would get this big. And then I saw it eating the burger." I gulped hard.

"Yeah, right." Luke snorted. "Did it have fries with that?"

I would have laughed out loud if one long finger of slime hadn't oozed over the top of the trash can and started dribbling down the side at that very minute. It was almost as if it knew where it was going.

Luke's face had turned a ghastly white, and his lips were moving, but nothing was coming out.

I didn't have time to worry about Luke. He would have to take care of himself. I was too busy watching the slime flowing across the floor toward the other side of the room.

I spotted a wadded-up candy wrapper

someone had pitched onto the floor. And sticking out of the wrapper was a half-eaten chocolate candy bar.

"Look!" I shouted.

Luke was already looking. His face was puckered up like he was going to cry. "It's . . . l—l—looking for . . . s—s—something to *eat*," he stammered.

I was feeling a little shaky myself as I watched it snake its way toward the discarded candy.

What happened next was so fast I almost missed it. The green slime shot out like an arrow and pulled the candy out of the crinkled wrapper. Then it snapped backward like a broken rubber band and disappeared—candy bar and all—into the ball of slime in the trash can.

I looked at Luke. He looked at me. Neither one of us could make a sound.

Chapter 5

"Let's get this thing out of here!" I cried, thinking fast. "Come on. Let's haul the can to the Dumpster. We can't wait for the janitor to do it after school. It may be as big as a rhino by then."

Luke gasped and gave me a look of disbelief. "Are you nuts?" he croaked. "Don't you think this would be a good time to run?"

The slime burped again, and the stench almost brought me to my knees. I wanted to

22

run just as much as Luke did, but I knew that I would have to stand my ground. My dad had spent four years in the air force. He said that in combat split-second decisions could uproot the course of history. In the next few days the future of Snodgrass would be changed forever.

"I'm the one who started this," I said to Luke in a shaky voice. "And I have to do what I can to end it."

"I respect you, Germ," he answered, "but I can't let you touch that stinking snot beast." His face was turning as green as the slime.

"Well, stupid," I retorted. "The can *does* have handles."

"But what if it comes after us, the way it went after that candy bar?" Luke whimpered.

"It won't, because we're not food," I said. I was surprised at how sure of myself I sounded.

I whipped open the door and stuck my head out into the hall to see if the coast was clear. It was. The bell must have already rung.

"Let's get moving," I said.

Luke was starting to get his color back, and he grabbed the handle on his side of the trash can as soon as I grabbed mine.

I looked down at the slime. It was bubbling away in there like a pot of green soup. The only odor left in the air was a faint whiff of chocolate.

I propped open the door with a foot and looked out into the hallway again. Still no one in sight. Motioning to Luke, I tried to lift my side of the can, but it was too heavy. Luke grunted as he tried to lift his side. He couldn't do it either.

"We'll just have to drag it," I said in a loud whisper.

Luke nodded and set his face in determination.

With him shoving from behind, I jerked on the handle, and together we dragged the heavy can into the hall. It was quiet as a tomb, and the scraping of the can across the floor echoed off the walls.

"Whew, this isn't going to be easy," Luke

said, keeping his voice low. "That Dumpster is on the other side of the building."

"So what? There's nothing we can do about it," I said, tugging harder. "We just have to hurry before someone sees us."

I should never have said anything about someone seeing us. It was probably a jinx. We were exactly even with the door to the media room when it flew open and Leanne Thomas came strutting out, her nose in the air and her arms full of papers. Leanne was in our class and she was always trying to kiss up to our teacher, Mr. Scanlon.

Just as she came through the door Luke gave a big shove, pushing me and the trash can straight into her. Leanne fell down and the photocopies she was taking to Mr. Scanlon flew into the air like a flock of white birds.

Naturally Leanne made the most of her accident.

"Look what you did!" she shouted at the top of her lungs. "You knocked me down! And look at my papers. They're everywhere.

Well, *you're* going to pick them up! All of them!"

I threw Luke a terrified look. The slime had spilled out onto the floor!

He grabbed a handful of soggy paper towels out of the can and spread them frantically over the green goo. I held my breath.

I had already begun to collect Leanne's papers off the floor. The hall was still empty.

"Here," I grumbled to Leanne. "Take your stupid papers."

Leanne didn't answer. She was staring at the trash can. Her mouth was wide open.

The paper towels were jiggling slightly as they slowly raised up past the rim of the can. Spots of green were popping up between them. *The slime was growing again!*

"Yeeewww! What *is* that green stuff?" she demanded. "And what are you doing with that trash can?"

"Who knows what it is?" I said hurriedly, stepping in front of the can and trying to hide it with my body as best I could. "The janitor asked us to empty it into the Dumpster, that's all. We're just doing him a favor. Tell Mr. Scanlon we'll come to class as soon as we're finished, okay?"

We didn't wait for her to answer. Luke gave the can a shove, and I pulled as hard as I could. Leanne was giving us a funny look as we pushed past her, but she didn't say anything else.

We didn't stop until we got to the Dumpster, and luckily we didn't meet anyone else in the halls. It took all our strength to get that can up onto our shoulders and heave it over the side of the Dumpster.

We didn't care that we'd probably be in trouble when we got back to class. We just fell onto the ground and panted with relief as soon as we saw the Dumpster lid close again. The slime was finally gone.

So why was my stomach still in knots?

Chapter

The next morning I came down late to the breakfast table. My mom was already walking out the door. She threw me a kiss, picked up her briefcase, and hurried out. Dad looked up from behind the newspaper. "How are you feeling?" he asked.

A lump rose in my throat. It had rained all night and I hadn't been able to sleep. Instead I listened to the raindrops knocking against the side of the house in the wind.

"I feel better," I said hoarsely.

Dad put down the paper. His eyes narrowed in a concerned frown. "Are you sure?" he asked. "If you're still sick, you should stay home today—soccer practice or no soccer practice."

Suddenly through the kitchen window behind Dad's head I saw Luke race into the driveway, waving his hands wildly. His face was whiter than it had been in the boys' bathroom yesterday.

I jumped to my feet and grabbed my book bag. "I have to go, Dad," I said, and without waiting for his answer I rushed out the back door.

Luke's lips were quivering. "You'r—r—r—e not gonna believ—v—v—ve this . . . I dunno if—f—f . . . it broke through everything. . . ."

"What are you talking about?" I demanded. A feeling of terrible dread washed over me as we walked toward school together.

"Some—somebody bro—bro—broke into the cafeteria last night," Luke choked out. "And they ate ev—ev—everything!"

"What do you mean?" I asked breathlessly. Maybe I *was* still a little sick. My eyes felt dry and tired. "Did they catch who did it?"

Luke shook his head so hard his pudgy cheeks bounced. "No—no—not yet. And ya—ya—ya know what I think?"

Before I could answer, Jason Dover and Mike Small came racing up. They were both talking fast and interrupting each other.

"You should see the cafeteria!" Jason shouted. "It's—"

"It's gross! I mean *really* gross!" Mike said, panting with excitement. "There's stuff smeared all over the floor and—"

"The windows are broken out—"

"Yeah! Right by the Dumpster. That's where the guy got in and—"

"And the doors are torn off the refrigerators—"

"And there's a yucky trail of slop leading straight back to the Dumpster," Mike said, collapsing against Jason and letting out a big sigh.

"The Dumpster?" I whispered. My heart was making so much noise, I almost couldn't hear my own voice.

"That's what I said," Mike muttered. "The cops are back there now. There's broken glass and junk all over."

"Come on," Jason said. "We'll show you."

Jason and Mike didn't even wait to see if Luke and I were coming. They took off toward the school, still talking excitedly.

My whole body was trembling.

"It couldn't be the slime, Luke," I said in a soft voice. But deep down I knew I was wrong. "How could it be?"

Luke was puffing too hard to say anything. But he didn't have to. I knew the answer myself. The slime had kept on growing after we chucked it into the Dumpster and went back to class. It had grown all afternoon, and maybe even found stuff in the trash to eat.

I shivered as hard as if the temperature were twenty below zero. I couldn't even picture slime big enough and strong enough to tear off a refrigerator door.

Two police cars nosed up to the Dumpster as soon as we turned the corner to the back of the school. The light bars were still flashing, and a voice crackled over the radio in one of the cars. Yellow crime-scene tape held back a mob of kids and teachers. Everybody was gawking hard and talking up a storm. Excited voices floated in the air.

"Pe—yew! It stinks!"

"I'd like to see the guy who did this. I'll bet his belly's as big as a house!"

"He ate so much he probably puked all over himself."

"Yeah, that's why it smells so gross!"

Everybody laughed.

Two police officers were milling around by the broken windows. One of them was poking through the mess on the ground with a stick. I heard the other one ask the janitor if he'd noticed anyone fooling around back there yesterday after school.

He said he hadn't.

My eyes homed in on the Dumpster. It was gross, all right. Long smears of mustard and ketchup ran up the side and stopped right under the lid. Next to that a jumble of spaghetti—looking like a writhing mass of snakes—clung to blood-red sauce. I couldn't identify a lot of the other stuff. It really did look like barf. A loudly buzzing swarm of flies was zooming in for the feast.

How big is the slime ball now? I wondered. *The size of a pickup truck? A house?*

Suddenly I felt a tug on my sleeve. I jumped like I'd been shot and whirled around. It was only Luke. He jerked his head toward the Dumpster. "What if it's still in there?" he asked in a panicky voice.

Luke's words hit me like a bolt of lightning. What if the slime ball *was* still in the Dumpster? And what if one of the policeofficers opened the lid and found it

33

in there? Was there any way they'd be able to figure out where it had come from?

My mouth went dry.

Chapter

7

The principal had come over the loudspeaker right after the bell to say that there would be no lunch in the cafeteria that day. He also said that anyone who had any information about the break-in should see him IMMEDIATELY.

I crouched low in my seat and felt the blood rising to my face. *No one will ever know that I'm connected to the slime,* I swore to myself. *No one except Luke. And he'll just have to keep this secret.*

The morning passed even more slowly

than usual. Yellow school buses lined the street in front of the school, ready to take kids who hadn't brought their lunches to McDonald's.

"Come on, Germ. If we hurry, we can get seats in the front of the bus. We'll be the first ones in McDonald's and the first ones to eat!" Luke said as we left the classroom. "I already know what I'm going to have—two Big Macs, two large fries, and an apple pie." He licked his lips and grinned at me.

I stared at him. How could he think of food at a time like this? "You go ahead," I said. "I'm not hungry."

"What do you mean, you're not hungry?" Luke demanded. "How often do we get a chance for a *good* meal around this place? You've got to be crazy!"

"I have something a little more important to think about," I said. I looked him straight in the eye. "I'm going out to that Dumpster."

"What for?" Luke asked. "The slime's gone. And anyway, there's nothing you can do about it."

"Maybe," I answered. "But I can't stop thinking about it. I won't be able to sleep until I know for sure that the slime is dead. Or at least far away from Snodgrass."

Luke's empty stomach let out a gigantic roar.

"Go on," I said. "I don't want you starving to death because of me."

The halls were emptying fast as kids poured out of the school and onto the buses. Luke was losing his chance for a front-row seat.

Suddenly a smile lit up his face. "I almost forgot. I don't have to go to McDonald's. I've got some candy bars in my desk."

He whirled around and raced back to his desk, scooping out three candy bars and a peanut butter cup. "Want one?" he asked halfheartedly.

I shook my head.

Luke looked relieved. He stuck the peanut butter cup and two of the candy bars in his pocket. Then he peeled open the last one and took a big bite.

As soon as the buses left we dashed into the hall. Except for the cleaning crew in the cafeteria, the school was empty. We didn't even have to tiptoe as we made our way out the door.

"What'll we do if the slime ball's still there?" Luke asked around a mouthful of chocolate.

"I don't know," I muttered. "We'll think of something."

"You can count me out if you're planning on moving it again." Luke shook his head. "I'm not messing with that thing *anymore!*"

We walked around the school to the Dumpster in the back, and I saw with relief that both the police cars were gone. The cafeteria window, where the slime ball had broken in, was boarded up, and the area around the Dumpster had been hosed off. Except for the boarded-up window, things looked pretty normal.

I took a deep breath, crouched low to the ground, and began advancing on the Dumpster. Luke popped another candy bar in his mouth and followed me. My hands were clammy, and my heart was in my mouth. What if it jumped out at us as soon as we got close?

I stopped when I got about three feet from the Dumpster and slowly stood up. I was eye level to the lid.

Luke stood up too. He was still chewing on his candy bar, and a thin stream of chocolate dribbled down his chin. He gave me a questioning look.

I swallowed hard. I didn't want to raise the lid. At least, not if the slime was still in there.

I had to do something or I would lose my nerve.

Just as I started to reach out for the lid, it bounced up and then shut tightly again.

I blinked and stared at it in horror. Had it really moved? Or had it been my imagination? It still looked closed.

My hand was shaking as I reached out again. Just then, the lid lifted slightly and a flash of green shot past my nose.

I staggered backward, looking for cover,

but the green arrow whizzed on by. To my horror, it was heading straight for Luke.

My mouth dropped open in terror as fingers of slime reached into his pocket and grabbed the rest of the candy. Then it zapped back into the Dumpster and the lid slammed shut again with a THUD!

Chapter

Luke looked like he'd seen a ghost. He clutched his shirt pocket where the candy had been and let out a moan. "Did—did—did you see that?" he stammered.

I tried to nod, but I was so scared my head just jerked up and down. A low rumbling noise was coming from the Dumpster. It was a sort of growl. Was the slime ball's stomach growling? Or maybe it sounded more like a snarl. Deep and heavy, like an animal about to spring.

I threw Luke a wild look. "Run!" I shouted.

The roar suddenly sounded louder.

I took off and dove around the corner of the school. Luke was right behind me. His teeth were chattering and sweat was pouring across his forehead.

I closed my eyes and listened hard. There was something familiar about that sound. I had heard it somewhere before.

I looked at Luke, and he looked at me. He must have thought it sounded familiar, too.

A big brown garbage truck was rolling onto the school grounds from the street behind the Dumpster and heading straight for it. The rumbling noise was coming from the truck!

For an instant I was relieved. Then I realized what was about to happen.

I watched the truck stop just in front of the Dumpster. The driver turned the truck slightly so that its long steel rods were lined up with the sides of the Dumpster. Then he drove slowly forward, latching the arms onto the huge metal bin. The motor whined as the arms started raising it into the air. When it reached the top, it spilled the garbage into the back of the truck.

I blinked as a flash of green slid out of the Dumpster and disappeared again into the pile of trash. It stank like crazy as the driver shifted gears and the arms gently set the Dumpster back on the ground. Then the truck backed off and slowly drove away.

"It'll get buried under tons of garbage at the landfill. We'll never see it again," I said hopefully.

Luke was still staring at the spot where the garbage truck had disappeared. "I hope you're right," he said.

Even though I knew the slime ball was gone, the sight of the empty Dumpster still gave me the shivers. "Come on," I said. "Let's get out of here."

By the time we got around front to the playground, the buses were unloading the kids who'd gone off for lunch. They spilled out of the big yellow buses, laughing and talking as they headed for the building.

"So how come you two weren't at McDonald's? You always buy your lunch."

I spun around to see Leanne Thomas standing there with both hands on her hips and a suspicious look on her face.

"What's it to you?" I asked with a snort. She could make me mad faster than any other kid I knew.

Leanne ignored my question. "Did you have *permission* to stay at school by yourself?" she demanded.

"We missed the buses," I said, scowling.

"Riiiiight," Leanne said. "Does Mr. Scanlon know that?"

I knew what she was getting at. Nothing would have made her happier than to rat on us.

Luke ran a hand through his thick red hair. "I forgot something in my desk, and we went back to get it. Do you want to write that down in your little notebook, Miss Know-it-all?" he retorted.

Leanne clicked her tongue against the back of her teeth for a minute, trying to think of a response. "What did you eat? Garbage from the Dumpster?" She threw back her head and laughed.

I winced. "Luke had some candy," I said lamely.

The bell rang and we all had to get to class. I was feeling pretty good when I sank into my seat. The slime ball was gone forever, and nobody knew about it but Luke and me.

And besides that, it was Friday. I had a whole weekend to forget about sneezing, snot, and slime balls. I could hardly wait!

Chapter

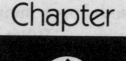

uke called right after breakfast on Saturday morning.

"What do you feel like doing today?" he asked. "Maybe we could ride our bikes to the park and go fishing in the lake. Our game's not till later this afternoon."

"Yeah, I guess so. . . ." I said without much enthusiasm.

"Got a better idea?"

"Naw . . . well, maybe," I said. I'd been awake most of the night, thinking about the slime ball. I dreamed that it was watching me through the window, from under the bed, and through the half-open closet door.

"Any century now," Luke said irritably. "You going to tell me your idea or am I supposed to read your mind?"

"You'll probably think this is silly, but maybe we should ride out to the city dump," I said. "You know, just to check things out. I mean, see if the slime ball got buried and stuff."

"Hey, cool!" Luke said excitedly. "Man, I love going out there! The place is full of crows and buzzards and even rats, and sometimes you can find neat stuff."

Fifteen minutes later we were on our bikes, heading for the dump. It was a long way outside of town, down a dirt road that wound through the woods. It had rained again and we had to swerve around the mud puddles in our path.

The dump itself was gross. Mountains of garbage were surrounded by a thick stench. Yellow bulldozers climbed through the haze, pushing and shoving the trash down into the piles. Overhead the sky was almost black with swarms of crows and buzzards, just like Luke had said. Sometimes they screamed and fought over pieces of old half-eaten food. Most of the time they just circled until they spotted a promising place to land and dig for food.

"Hey, look! There's a TV set," Luke cried. He was pointing to the next mountain over from where we had parked our bikes. "I wonder if it still works? And here's a skateboard! All it needs is wheels!"

I ignored Luke and swatted the flies that were buzzing around my face as I studied the landfill. All the mountains of garbage looked pretty much the same. They were jumbles of broken boards and crumpled boxes and tin cans and stuff I couldn't even identify. There was no way to tell where the trash truck had dumped the load from the school.

"Yikes! What did I tell you? There's a rat!" Luke shrieked suddenly.

He was jumping up and down and

pointing straight out in front of us, but when I looked, the rat was already gone.

"Come on, Luke. Help me look for the slime," I grumbled.

Luke threw a few nervous glances toward the spot where the rat had been. Then he swiped at a fly and said, "Okay, where do you want me to look?"

"Anywhere. Look for anything green," I insisted. "Just help me find it. I've got to make sure it's here."

"If we do find the slime, we're not going to be able to do anything about it," Luke said.

"I know that," I snapped. I hadn't slept or eaten much in days. I was exhausted, but I had to keep looking. The slime was haunting my dreams. I could think of nothing else.

We trudged over the mountains, silent except for the crunching of the garbage underfoot. A couple of times guys driving bulldozers yelled at us to get out of the dump, but we just kept on poking into the junk and looking for signs of the slime.

"I give up," Luke muttered a while later. He wiped sweat off his face and gave me a disgusted look. "I'm going home. We've been looking for at least an hour, and we haven't found a thing. Even if it's out here, it's probably smashed to smithereens by now."

I was beginning to think Luke was right. Besides, it had to be buried under tons of stuff. How could two kids ever find it?

Just then the garbage under my feet shifted. I swayed and caught myself just in time to keep from falling.

Luke gave me a funny look. "What happened?"

I looked carefully at the junk I was standing on. Old magazines. A paint can. Ragged curtains. Nothing green and slimy.

"Ready to go?" Luke called over his shoulder. He was already hurrying down the mound. "I *definitely* am."

But I didn't want to leave—not without learning more about the slime.

Suddenly I felt the garbage under my feet

shift again, only this time it pushed me straight upward. I gasped, wheeling my arms in the air to keep my balance as the whole mountain began to tremble and expand. Deep inside I could hear it groan.

"Whooooaaaa!" I let out a frightened screech.

Below me I could see Luke's terrified face. "Run! It's coming after us!"

I felt myself tumbling head over heels down the side of the garbage mountain. I slammed to a stop at the bottom of the heap. I was on my stomach, and my face was smushed into a rotting head of cabbage.

The mountain of trash suddenly became still again. Only a lone tin can clattered down the side and bumped to a stop against my leg.

I lay there, spitting out rotten cabbage and listening. The groaning had stopped. All I could hear was Luke's panting, the birds' screaming above me, and the pounding of my own heart.

Chapter

Luke slept over, and we were watching cartoons in the family room after breakfast the next morning when the show was interrupted by a news bulletin.

"Good morning," a gray-haired anchorman began. "This is a bulletin just in to the channel seventy-three news center. Local authorities have closed the city's landfill as concern builds over possible toxic contamination.

"Yesterday afternoon workers became

alarmed when one of the large mounds of trash began expanding on its own. No immediate explanation could be found for the rapid growth of the refuse pile, and authorities fear lethal chemicals could be buried inside.

"I repeat! The local landfill has been closed until further notice because of possible toxic contamination, and the police are urging everyone to stay away. We'll bring you more details as they become available. Now we return you to your regularly scheduled program."

I looked at Luke in alarm. "It's out there and it's growing," I said. Fear sent little prickles down my spine.

"Yeah, and they think it's toxic contamination," Luke said. He grinned impishly and added, "Maybe we should tell them it's just snot."

"Cut it out, Luke. This is serious." I felt close to tears. "We have to do something!"

"Do something about what?" My dad was standing in the doorway. He was wearing his golfing outfit: yellow-and-green-striped shorts and his favorite T-shirt, the light blue one that said BERNIE'S ICE CREAM.

I jumped off my seat on the sofa. "Oh, just a project for school," I said, forcing myself to smile.

"Well, you boys shouldn't be doing schoolwork on a beautiful day like today," my dad said. "The rain's finally let up. It's a crime to stay inside when the weather's so gorgeous out."

I continued to grin weakly, but Luke and I were both silent.

My dad looked from my face to Luke's. "I have an idea," he said. "Why don't you two come out to the public golf course with me? We can play a few rounds and then go to Bernie's for an ice cream cone."

Good old Dad, I thought. *He knows something's wrong and he thinks an ice cream cone can fix it. He'd be so disappointed with me if he knew the truth.*

A tear rolled out of the corner of my eye. I turned away and wiped it off quickly.

"Is your cold still bothering you?" my dad asked.

I sniffed. "Nah," I said. "I feel fine now."

"You know, I think we might just take you up on your offer," Luke said to my dad. "My game could definitely stand some work."

I kicked Luke under the coffee table, trying to signal to him that we couldn't go golfing. We had to figure out a way to stop the slime.

"I don't think that's such a good idea—" I began, but Dad cut me off.

"Your schoolwork can wait," he said. "We haven't been spending enough time together lately and that's something that we have to change. Right now."

When Dad spoke in that tone of voice, I knew there was no point arguing with him.

"I wonder what sundae specials Bernie's has today," Luke was saying, his mouth open in a huge grin.

I sighed, but actually I was kind of glad to get away from the whole slime problem.

Maybe Luke's right, I thought. *Maybe there isn't anything we can do about it. And now that the sanitation department has moved in, I'm sure they'll be able to handle it. I mean, this can't be the only time they've had to deal with snot, right?*

Luke and I got into the backseat of Dad's old Buick station wagon and we drove out to the highway toward the golf course. Just as we turned out of town, though, the traffic began to bottleneck. There seemed to be some sort of demonstration going on at the junction where the road to the Snodgrass dump split off.

Police cars blocked off the entrance to the road and an angry mob was gathering.

"Hey, I saw how that thing swelled up!" someone shouted from the front row.

"Why aren't the police doing anything?" someone else yelled. "I want some answers!"

"Yeah! Who's going to keep my family safe if it is toxic waste?"

Dad slowly made his way around the cars that had stopped to watch the demonstration. Finally we reached the golf course and pulled into a space in the parking lot.

As Dad got his golfing equipment out of the trunk, Luke and I wandered around to the end of the parking lot. From there we could see the entire golf course stretched out before us. For the first time in days I felt relaxed. The bright green lawn glistened in the sun and the water in the ponds rippled gently as a soft breeze blew.

But wait—one of the ponds at the far edge of the course was breaking into tall, sharp waves. It looked like something big had gotten into the water and was splashing around.

I gasped and grabbed Luke's arm, pointing toward the pond. "What the—" Luke turned in the direction I was pointing and stopped short in midsentence.

A woman who had hit her ball near the water was walking toward it. Then suddenly from the depths of the pond the slime, now as big as a house, reared up, like a huge stench-filled Loch Ness monster. The woman clapped her hand over her nose and began to run.

The whole golf course was shaking as if an earthquake had hit. It was unbelievable. Across the course people stopped playing and just leaned on their clubs and stared.

A few hawks were circling above the pond—probably drawn by the smell of rotting food. One of them dove low over the water and suddenly the slime began to tremble more violently. Pieces of garbage that it had picked up at the dump were shaking loose and splashing down. Then, while everyone watched in horror, the slime reared up again. It stretched itself out into a long, slimy arm and shot upward, grabbing the squawking hawk and sucking it back inside the mound of goop.

BURP!

The slime receded back into the pond and silence fell over the green again. I could see my dad standing in the far corner of the parking lot, his mouth agape. Suddenly all across the course people exploded with panic. Everyone started to run.

Chapter

11

"**L**et's get out of here!" I shouted to Luke. But he was already dashing toward the highway.

"Germ, hurry!" he cried. He looked as if he might die of fright any second.

I hesitated for a minute. I couldn't see my dad through the crowds of people running to their cars. Then I heard the wail of sirens. Several police cars and a fire truck were already pulling up. They roared past with their lights flashing and spinning.

Luke had paused to wait for me. We both

coughed and spit as thick dust from their tires fogged the air. A minute later the sirens faded and the air began to clear.

I looked for my father, but his car was gone. *He probably had to clear the space for the police cars,* I thought. I glanced at Luke. He had a dazed expression on his face.

"What's going to happen now?" he asked.

"The whole world is about to learn about the green slime," I answered. "Now even the police have seen it. What am I going to do, Luke?"

"What do you mean, what are *you* going to do?" he asked.

"I started the whole thing," I said solemnly. "I have to find a way to stop it before things get any worse."

Luke squinted at me and shook his head. "I don't think there's any way you can stop it," he said. "I mean, how could you? That thing's feeding on birds! Do you understand what that means? It eats *meat,* like a big old dinosaur. And the more it eats, the bigger it gets!"

I groaned. "That's why I have to stop it," I said. "Or Snodgrass is going to go down in history as the town that was eaten by snot."

Just then thunder rumbled in the distance. That meant we'd probably get soaked walking home, I thought absently. Just what I needed.

"Let's get going," I said. But Luke was frozen to the spot. All the color had drained out of his face.

I swallowed hard. "What's the matter, Luke?" I asked nervously.

"L—l—l—ook," he stammered, and pointed over my shoulder back toward the golf course.

I was afraid to look behind me, but I knew I had to, so I turned around as slowly as I could. My mouth went dry. My heart pounded in my ears.

The mountain of slime was a mass of quivering green garbagey gunk. Green oozed out everywhere and came together in one liquid mass to roll over the banks of the pond like lava down a volcano.

It buried the abandoned golf carts in snotty goo. Like a tidal wave of split-pea soup, it washed over the chain-link fence that surrounded the course and rolled on down the road toward the spot where Luke and I clung to each other in terror.

"Germ! It's coming after us!" Luke shrieked as he sprang into a run.

I took off after him, running as hard as I could—as if my life depended on it.

Chapter

12

My lungs felt like they were going to burst, but I kept moving as fast as I could. I could hear the low rumbling of the slime falling back. *It can't keep up with us!* I realized.

By the time we made it back to town, we had left the slime far behind us. Word had already spread that something sinister was going on at the city dump and at the Snodgrass public golf course. Drivers returning from the outskirts of town had stopped their cars along the streets to describe to total strangers how the mountain of garbage was swelling up as big as a skyscraper and how it had broken out of the dump.

Pandemonium was breaking loose everywhere when we ran up Main Street a few minutes later. People were rushing in all directions. CLOSED signs suddenly appeared on storefronts. As we pedaled past the park a frantic mother grabbed up her toddler and hurried for home.

"Boys, get in the house! Lock your doors!" she shouted over her shoulder.

My heart was racing, too. I thought I would explode with panic.

"This is all my fault! What am I going to do?" I shouted to Luke. "How am I going to stop that stuff?"

"I don't know, Germ," he shouted back. "But we've got to think of something and think of it fast."

He would never know how relieved I felt to hear him say "we." Even if we couldn't stop the slime from rolling into town, at least he wasn't going to desert me.

"Let's go to my house," I called breathlessly. My chest was aching from running so hard. I was panting like crazy, and a sharp pain screamed in my side. "If I can make it that far," I added, just above a whisper.

Just a little bit farther, I promised myself as I whizzed up the street and around a corner. I let out a little cry of joy when I saw my house up ahead. Luke was only a couple of seconds behind me. The driveway was empty, which meant that Dad hadn't returned yet.

Taking the steps three at a time, I banged open the front door. "Mom! Anybody home?"

The only answer was a hearty "Woof!" coming from the kitchen. The next thing I saw was a streak of yellow as Sunshine, my golden retriever, bounded into the room and covered my face with sloppy kisses. Next she attacked Luke, slurping him with her huge pink tongue.

"Down, girl. Down," I said, and called out

for Mom again. Maybe Dad would have called her. But there was still no answer. That was funny. She wouldn't be at work on Sunday, and she had been here when we left for the dump.

"Got anything to eat?" Luke asked.

"How can you even think of food at a time like this?" I shot back.

"I can't concentrate on an empty stomach and I'm *starved!*" Luke said. "Don't forget, I was expecting ice cream."

I shrugged and headed for the kitchen. If eating something would help Luke concentrate so we could think up a way to get rid of the slime, it sounded like a good idea to me.

I opened the fridge, pulling out sandwich stuff and half an apple pie. My hands were shaking so hard I almost dropped the pie. Sunshine danced eagerly around my feet.

I set everything down and glanced around for Luke. He was standing in front of the TV on the countertop, which he'd switched on when he came in the room.

"If you want a sandwich, you have to make it yourself," I grumbled.

"Uh-oh, Germ. Come here quick. You gotta see this," he said in a deadly serious voice.

I took a deep breath before I looked at the TV.

A woman with a microphone in her hand was standing in a field. She glanced nervously back over her shoulder and then straight into the camera.

"A terrifying phenomenon is occurring behind me and just over those hills," she said. "A sea of what appears to be green slime is slowly rolling over the countryside. It has grown to the size of twelve city blocks and is moving at the rate of approximately six feet per hour. Authorities do not know the composition of the slime at this time, and there is fear it may contain toxic chemicals that could prove harmful to human beings. It was first noticed yesterday by workers at the local landfill when trash mounds began to grow larger and larger on their own."

She paused, and Luke and I looked at each other.

The reporter was speaking again. "In a desperate attempt to stop the advancing sea of slime on its steady march toward the small town of Snodgrass, authorities have called in the National Guard."

"The National Guard!" Luke and I cried in unison.

"A spokesman for the Guard told this reporter just moments ago that tanks and helicopters are being rushed to the scene."

I began stomping around the room. "There has to be some way to get rid of it," I insisted. "After all, it was just a big glob of snot."

Luke gave me a skeptical look. "Yeah? Then how come it keeps growing all by itself? And how come it eats things like hamburger and candy and now birds!"

"I wish I knew," I said, burying my face in my hands.

Suddenly the reporter's voice caught my attention again.

"This bulletin has just been handed to me," she said.

"Listen up, Luke," I cried. "This could be important."

"A sixth grader from Snodgrass Middle School named Leanne Thomas has just told police that she has information about the slime and believes she knows who is responsible."

My heart thudded to a complete stop. "Leanne Thomas?" I gasped.

Luke threw me a worried look. "Yeah," he whispered back. "What do you think she knows?"

The reporter's voice cut in again. "Now we switch you back to the studio, where anchorman Bob Austin is conducting a live interview. Bob?"

The picture changed to a studio shot and a tall, thin man with a dark mustache looked soberly into the camera.

I tried to swallow as I waited to see what would happen next, but my Adam's apple was shaking so hard my spit wouldn't go down.

70

"Thank you, Traci. I have here with me twelve-year-old Leanne Thomas."

I watched in horror as the shot widened and Leanne Thomas grinned into the camera.

"Good afternoon, Mr. Austin. It's a pleasure to be here," she said in her prissiest voice.

"I understand you shared some information about the slime with the police. Could you tell us what that information was?"

Leanne stuck her nose into the air and said importantly, "On Thursday, I saw two boys in my school dragging a trash can to the Dumpster. I didn't think much about it at the time, but now that I remember, it was full of stuff that looked exactly like *green slime,* only there wasn't so much of it. I'm sure that was it, because the Dumpster always gets emptied into the landfill, and that's where the slime started to grow."

"That's fascinating, Leanne," Bob Austin said. "Do you know the names of those boys?"

"I certainly do," she answered immediately. My heart stopped. "Jeremy Wilson and Luke Damato. Jeremy also answers to the name of 'Germ.' I told the police, and they're probably looking for them now!"

Just then there was a loud pounding on the front door.

Chapter

"**C**ops! Let's get outta here!" I shouted. "Come on! The back door!"

Sunshine was running around in circles, barking like crazy. The minute she heard the words *back door* she made a beeline toward it, and all three of us squeezed out at the same time.

I streaked through the backyard and ducked between a couple of houses, not stopping until I had put three blocks between me and my own house.

"Slow down," Luke croaked. He was

huffing and puffing, and his pudgy face was bright red. Even his ears were pink.

I was out of breath too, so I leaned against a telephone pole and waited for him to catch up. Sunshine trotted along, panting happily, her big pink tongue lolling out one side of her mouth.

I glanced around nervously. There were no cars on the street and nobody in sight. Everybody was probably locked in their houses because of the green slime.

"I wonder how long the cops will keep knocking on my door before they figure out nobody's home?" I asked, and shot a terrified glance in the direction we'd just come.

"They're probably at my house, too," Luke said, trembling. "What do you think they'll do to us if they catch us?"

"They'll pump us for information about the green slime and where it came from," I said, gulping hard. I'd seen lots of police shows on TV so I knew what to expect. "They'll probably put us in different rooms and not let us go to sleep until one of us breaks and tells them what they want to know."

Luke frowned. "But we don't know anything about the slime except that it started out as a glob of snot. We don't have any idea how to stop it from growing any bigger. Maybe we should just give ourselves up and explain what we know to the police."

I glared at him. "Are you crazy? Do you really think the cops would believe us if we told them it was only snot? They've called out the National Guard! They're not going to believe a story like that."

Luke sighed and crumpled inward like a balloon losing air. "I guess you're right."

Suddenly I had the jitters. "We'd better keep moving," I said. "We've got to find a place to hide and find it *quick*!"

Luke nodded. "How about the woods?"

"Don't be stupid. That's where the green slime is." I snorted. "We've got to find a better place than that."

I chewed on my bottom lip and racked my

brain. There weren't very many places to hide in Snodgrass. Then I thought of it. The most perfect place in the world!

"The school!" I shouted. "This is Sunday. There won't be anybody there until tomorrow morning. Nobody will ever think to look for us there, and it will give us some time to try to figure out what to do!"

"Yeah, but how'll we get in?" Luke asked. "The doors will all be locked."

I gave him a sly grin. "The slime broke into the cafeteria, remember? The window's just boarded up."

Luke's face lit up. "Good idea! We can pry it open, squeeze inside, and then board it up again. Nobody will ever find us there!"

"Woof!" Sunshine wagged her tail excitedly.

I whirled around to start off toward the school—and froze. A police car was crawling around the corner, heading in our direction.

"Duck!" I whispered, and dove into a big bush beside the nearest house.

An instant later Luke and Sunshine were

both beside me. Sunshine was panting in my ear as I peered out between the leaves. The police car was slowly moving toward us. Mounted on the roof of the car was a loudspeaker, which crackled to life as it got closer.

"ATTENTION, CITIZENS! BE ON THE LOOKOUT FOR TWO TWELVE-YEAR-OLD BOYS WANTED BY THE POLICE FOR QUESTIONING REGARDING THE SLIME THAT IS MENACING THE TOWN. THEY ARE: LUKE DAMATO AND JEREMY WILSON. WILSON ALSO GOES BY THE NAME 'GERM'! NOTIFY THE POLICE IMMEDIATELY IF YOU SEE THESE BOYS!"

I watched the patrol car move slowly past us and on down the street. Its blaring loudspeaker sent chills racing through me.

Luke's chin was quivering. "How are we going to make it to the school now?"

Chapter

As the noise from the loudspeaker gradually died away, I peered nervously around the quiet neighborhood. Behind every window there could be people waiting to jump out and drag us down to the police station. Maybe some of them even had binoculars to help them see farther. There was no way we could move out from behind the bushes now.

Suddenly I missed Sunshine. I glanced around, but the big yellow dog was nowhere to be seen.

I nudged Luke, who was leaning forward, staring out through the foliage. "Is Sunshine over there with you?"

"Uh-uh," Luke replied. "I don't know where—" He stopped and pointed to the middle of the street.

There was Sunshine, loping happily away from us. She crossed to the other side of the street and sank into a patch of shade on somebody's lawn, stopping once to sniff a blade of grass.

"Sunshine," I hissed. "Get back over here."

Luke looked at me in alarm. "Be careful. Somebody might hear you," he warned.

"I've got to get her back here," I said. Then I stuck my head out of the bushes and yelled a little louder. "Sunshine! Come here, girl!"

She tossed a bored look in my direction. Then she stood up and ambled off, moving farther away from where Luke and I were hiding.

"That stupid dog!" I mumbled in

frustration. "I've got to get her back! She's not used to being out by herself. She'll get lost—or worse."

"You can't go after her," Luke insisted. "Somebody'll see you! Maybe she'll come back."

"But what if she doesn't?" I asked, a lump forming in my throat.

Just then another sound caught my attention.

Ka–whack! Ka–whack! Ka–whack!

"What the—?" Luke cried.

KA–WHACK! KA–WHACK! KA–WHACK! KA–WHACK!

Whatever it was, was getting closer. And louder! We stuck our heads out of the bushes and sucked in our breath in surprise. Helicopters! There were dozens of them, blackening the sky like a swarm of mosquitoes, and they were heading in the direction of the city golf course.

"Wow! It's the National Guard!" Luke said in awe. "Would you look at all those choppers?"

"I see 'em," I muttered. Suddenly a brilliant idea popped into my head. "Everybody in town sees them, too! There's never been anything like this over Snodgrass before, so nobody will even notice us. If we hurry, we can make it to the school! Come on, Luke. It's now or never!" I shouted over the drone of the helicopter blades.

Luke popped up through the branches with a big grin on his face. "Let's do it!"

"Follow me!" I yelled, and took off like a rocket. I whistled for Sunshine, and she wheeled around and streaked after Luke and me. "Atta girl," I yelled, and kept on running.

We raced between houses. We cut through carports, stopping and flattening ourselves against the nearest building whenever we spotted a police car coming our way. The message blaring out of the loudspeakers was almost drowned out by the sound of the helicopters, but we could hear it just the same.

"ATTENTION, CITIZENS! BE ON THE

LOOKOUT FOR TWO TWELVE-YEAR-OLD BOYS—"

Each time a patrol car came creeping by, I would grab Sunshine and hold her muzzle tightly shut to keep her from barking when she heard my name.

"THEY ARE: LUKE DAMATO AND JEREMY WILSON. WILSON ALSO GOES BY THE NAME 'GERM'!—"

Just as the sound of the helicopters died away, we reached the school. The red brick building had never looked so good to me in my life.

"I just hope they haven't fixed the cafeteria window since Friday," Luke said. "Of course, it would be the first time they fixed anything in under twelve months."

We ducked around to the back and hurried to the cafeteria window. It was still boarded up.

"This is going to be a piece of cake," I assured Luke as I inspected the boards. "The nails aren't even hammered in very tightly. Let's find a stick or something to pry it open with."

Luke nodded, and we both got busy scouring the area behind the school for anything that could pry open the window. There wasn't much to be found. A few school papers caught on twigs and flapping in the breeze. An empty soda can. Somebody's gym sock with a hole in the toe.

The whole time we were looking, I kept one eye peeled for a patrol car and one ear strained to hear the loudspeakers again.

Suddenly I heard someone talking, but the voice wasn't coming over any loudspeaker. It was just around the corner of the school and coming our way.

"I just *loved* being on TV, Officer. Did you see the show?"

"No, and what's more, you shouldn't be out on the streets with that dangerous slime headed this way. There's no way to know what it's going to do. I'll give you a ride home in my patrol car. It's parked a couple of streets over."

Luke and I looked at each other in horror. Leanne Thomas! And a policeman! If they found us, we'd be dead meat! But where could we hide?

The thought horrified me. Wasn't that where all the trouble had started in the first place? But still, it was the only safe place we could get to in time.

The Dumpster.

Luke must have read my mind because he immediately made a face and shook his head wildly.

"There's no place else," I whispered. "Hurry! They'll be here any second!"

While I grabbed Sunshine, Luke held his nose with one hand and raised the Dumpster's lid with the other.

Chapter

Luke and I scrambled into the Dumpster as fast as we could, pulling Sunshine in along with us. Then we lowered the lid, leaving only a slit so we could look out. The smell of old garbage made me gag, but at least nothing new had been put into the Dumpster since the garbage truck had emptied it out on Friday.

We had barely gotten inside when Leanne and the policeman came around the corner. Leanne was still yakking away about being on TV.

"I didn't even have stage fright," she bragged. "And people have been calling my parents all day to say how natural I looked and how intelligent I sounded."

That made me gag even worse.

Then, just when they got even with the Dumpster, Sunshine began to squirm. She was trying to break out of my arms, and her paws made little scratching sounds on the metal as she struggled.

I raised her ear and whispered into it, "Cut it out, Sunshine!"

She gave me a mournful look and sat still for a minute. Then she started squirming again. But Leanne and the policeman had already turned the corner again.

"That was a close one," Luke said, wiping the sweat off his forehead.

"Yeah? Well, I kept her quiet, didn't I? Open the lid so we can get out of here," I said. "This place is making me sick to my stomach."

"You and me both," he replied, and heaved up the lid.

I took a deep breath of fresh air and had bent over to lift Sunshine out of the Dumpster when something in the corner by my foot caught my eye. Something green.

"Luke," I said, taking a step backward. "Look at this."

He looked annoyed. "Let's just get out of here, okay?"

"I think you'd better look," I said. Fear was growing in the pit of my stomach.

Luke glanced down and let out a wail. "Oh, no. No. It can't be."

"It is," I said dryly.

"More slime!"

"I bet it's a little piece that got left behind when the garbage truck emptied the Dumpster," I said, leaning over to get a better look.

It was slime, all right. A hunk of it about the size of a softball. Suddenly I had an idea.

"As soon as we can get into the school, I'm coming back to get it," I said.

Luke's mouth dropped open. "Are you crazy? It grows, you know. And eats stuff!"

"I know that," I insisted. "But if we have a piece of it to study and experiment on, maybe we can figure out how to destroy it. It's our only chance."

Luke climbed out of the Dumpster, looking disgusted. "It's your snot. *You* study it and *you* experiment on it all you want to. Just count me out."

Before I could argue anymore, I heard a voice coming over a loudspeaker again. It sounded like it was in front of the school.

"ATTENTION, JEREMY WILSON AND LUKE DAMATO. IF YOU CAN HEAR THIS, PLEASE CONTACT THE SNODGRASS POLICE IMMEDIATELY. I REPEAT, GERM WILSON AND LUKE DAMATO. PLEASE CONTACT THE SNODGRASS POLICE WITHOUT DELAY REGARDING THE SLIME THAT IS INVADING THE TOWN. THIS IS AN EMERGENCY!"

"Why don't we give ourselves up," Luke growled. "If they find out we don't know anything, maybe they'll leave us alone."

"Fat chance," I replied. "Don't you see,

Luke? Our only hope is to figure out how to destroy the slime before it destroys Snodgrass. Then we'll go to the police. I promise."

Luke didn't say anything for a minute. I could see he was thinking it over.

"But how are we going to study it and experiment on it?" he asked, shaking his head. "How will we figure out what to do? We're just a couple of kids."

"I don't know yet," I said. "But there's a science lab in the school and a whole library full of books. Don't you see? It's the best place to be in the whole town!"

Another car with a loudspeaker was coming closer. This time the voice sounded familiar. "JEREMY, PLEASE LISTEN TO ME. YOU'RE A GOOD KID. I KNOW YOU'D NEVER DO ANYTHING BAD ON PURPOSE. BUT PLEASE, TURN YOUR- SELF IN. WE CAN HELP YOU. MAYBE I HAVEN'T BEEN AS GOOD A FATHER AS I COULD HAVE BEEN. . . ."

His voice trailed off as the police car

passed the school. I wanted to jump out of the Dumpster and run over to my dad in the car. I wanted him to tell me that this was all just a nightmare—to make it go away. But at the same time I was angry.

It's not as if I wanted my snot, of all the possible snot in Snodgrass, to rage out of control. So I took some nasty cold medication. Who knows if that's even what started the slime in the first place?

But underneath the anger I felt a growing sense of despair. The whole town of Snodgrass had turned on me. Even my own father.

I t didn't take long to pry the boards away from the cafeteria window and sneak inside the school. Sunshine's barks echoed off the walls as she bounded through the empty halls.

I made sure the coast was clear before I returned to the Dumpster to get the slime. Then I took a mixing bowl and a big spoon from the kitchen so that I wouldn't have to touch the gooey gob. I climbed into the Dumpster and knelt beside it. It had grown again in the short time Luke and I had been gone. Now it was the size of a grapefruit. It must have been only a speck when it was left in the Dumpster or it would have grown faster than this.

"I wonder how big the other slime is by now?" I muttered to myself. "Is it getting close to town yet? And what is it eating now?" I shuddered, not wanting to think about that, and scooped the slime into the bowl.

When I climbed back inside the cafeteria, Luke was in a frenzy, opening cabinet doors and slamming them shut.

"That stupid slime ate everything and I'm starved!" he cried. "It's almost suppertime, and I haven't had anything to eat since breakfast."

I hadn't eaten much in days and I was starting to feel hungry, too.

Luke opened another cabinet and his face lit up.

"Crackers!" he cried, pulling out a big box of saltines. "Now at least I won't starve!"

"Let's go to the media center and look up

slime in the big dictionary. We can eat while we work," I said. When I saw Luke's skeptical look, I added, "It's a start, right?"

I picked up the bowl of slime, and Luke grabbed the box of crackers and followed me down the hall, munching as he went.

I was heading for the dictionary that was kept on a tall stand by the window when I noticed the television set in a console by the wall. Teachers used it to show videos to their classes.

"Hey, maybe there's something about the slime on the news," I cried. "Maybe the helicopters and the tanks were able to destroy it!"

"Yeah, turn it on," Luke said.

I punched the power button and the screen flashed to life. The same reporter we'd seen earlier in the day was standing at the outskirts of town beside a sign that said:

WELCOME TO SNODGRASS
POP. 6,000

Behind her a sea of green was moving forward like a tidal wave.

93

She threw a nervous glance over her shoulder and then began speaking in a trembling voice. "National Guard tanks and helicopters have made no progress whatsoever in stopping the advance of the slime that is threatening to engulf Snodgrass. They've fired their cannons and machine guns at it, but the bullets have gone right through and don't seem to have inflicted any permanent damage on the slime.

"At this moment the slime is less than the length of a football field away from the outskirts of the tiny town. It is growing bigger and gaining strength as it gobbles up birds and rodents and other small woodland creatures in its path and is expected to reach Snodgrass in less than an hour. All citizens have been ordered to get out of town immediately!"

I gulped hard. I didn't like the idea of me and Luke being the only ones left in town.

"In other developments, the two twelve-year-old boys who may hold the key to solving the mystery of the slime are still at large."

A pair of pictures flashed on the screen. They were Luke's and my school pictures. I gulped. We were honest-to-goodness fugitives!

"In spite of a massive search by local police," she was saying, "Jeremy Wilson and Luke Damato have not been seen since early this morning, when they ran away from the scene of the slime at Snodgrass Public Golf Course. Authorities fear that the boys may have been eaten."

Luke's chin dropped to his chest and the box of crackers crashed to the floor. "Oh, my gosh, Germ! They think it ate us!"

I stared at the screen, not hearing anything else the reporter was saying. I was looking at the massive wave of slime behind her. It had grown so huge that it covered everything as far as the eye could see. Barns had been flattened! Trees had been mowed down like blades of grass! It was eating everything that got in its way, even small animals!

A wave of nausea crashed over me.

I stiffened straight as a poker as I played the reporter's words over and over in my mind. *Authorities fear that the boys may have been eaten.*

The slime was eating humans.

Chapter

17

I tried to ignore the steady line of cars streaming past the window on their way out of town as I ran my fingers down the words in the dictionary, looking for *slime*.

"Here it is," I said, reading out loud. "*Slime,* number one, 'soft, moist earth.' That's not it," I said, skipping down the line of definitions. "Here, number four, 'a mucous'—that's it!" I kept on reading. "'Thick, syrupy, and sticky substance exuding from the body.'"

"That's it, all right. Snot!" Luke said. "Does it say how to get rid of it?"

I shook my head. "Maybe if I look up *snot,*" I said hopefully.

I turned a few pages and read the definition. "'*Snot,* mucus discharged from the nose.'"

"Is that all?" Luke asked.

"That's it," I said dejectedly. "Except for the second definition: 'an offensive or contemptible person.' I guess I must be a snot, because that's how I feel right now. If I hadn't sneezed in the first place, we wouldn't be in this mess."

I glanced back out the window. The stream of cars leaving town was even bigger than before. A picture of my parents' faces flashed in my mind. They must be going crazy, thinking I was dead. Were they getting out of town, too? I hoped so, but I knew I couldn't take the time to find out right now.

Luke was scanning the rows of books lining the shelves of the media center. "Maybe we can find a book—"

"What are we doing?" I snapped. The hugeness of the slime problem was suddenly getting through to me. "If all anybody had to do to figure out how to get rid of the slime was look it up in a book, then somebody else would have figured it out by now. We're wasting our time."

Luke blinked hard and then nodded. "I guess you're right."

"Of course I'm right. This isn't ordinary slime. Even the National Guard can't do anything about it, which means we're on our own, Luke. We're going to have to figure this out by ourselves. Let's try the science lab."

"Okay, you get the slime and I'll get the crackers," he said.

Turning around, we gasped in unison. While we were talking, the slime had puffed up until it could slide over the edge of the bowl and drop a ropelike arm onto the floor. Next it stretched out the arm and moved it in a straight line toward a couple of Luke's crackers, which were scattered on the floor.

I watched in horror as fingers of thick green goo made a beeline toward the food.

"We've got to stop it!" Luke cried. "We can't let it get any bigger!"

But the slime was too fast. It hit the crackers like a striking snake! Then as suddenly as it had hit the crackers, it shuddered hard and recoiled.

HISSSSSS!

A wisp of smoke rose above the slimy arm as it hung in midair for an instant and then crumpled to the floor.

"Did you see that? What happened?" Luke whispered.

All I could do was shake my head and stare in astonishment at the limp ribbon of green stretched out on the floor in front of us. Slowly I reached down and picked up the cracker, turning it over in my hand.

Then I noticed something on the floor next to where the cracker had been. It looked like a tiny square of green paper at first, and it was the same color green as the slime. I did a double take and reached for it, but the instant I touched it, it turned to ash and fell apart in my hand.

Suddenly the remaining slime at my feet began to rock back and forth and stretch, like it was waking up from a long nap. I jumped back as it started to grow and move around.

"Look out!" I shouted.

But the slime wasn't headed toward Luke, and it wasn't headed for me. It was slithering across the floor like a runaway freight train, zooming straight for Sunshine, who was curled up in a corner on the other side of the room, sound asleep!

Chapter

"Sunshine! Look out!" I screamed. My heart pounded. I remembered the reporter saying the slime was getting its strength from eating small woodland animals. Now this piece was after Sunshine! I couldn't let it get her!

The big yellow dog opened her eyes halfway and gave me a bored look. Then she lowered her head again, sighed softly, and went back to sleep.

"Sunshine! Get out of there!" I screamed again. "The slime's going to eat you!"

"Come on, girl! You can do it!" Luke urged.

The green slime was between us and the dog, silently flowing toward her. Luke and I both started grabbing books off the nearest table and pitching them at the slime. But they bounced off uselessly and hit the floor.

Suddenly the dog sensed the danger. She raised her head, pricked her ears, and started to growl.

The slime had slowed down now, creeping closer as if it was trying to sneak up on her.

"WOOF! WOOF!" Sunshine was on her feet, baring her fangs at the advancing slime.

It had totally cut off the path between her and us. In fact, in just a few more inches Sunshine would be boxed into a corner with no way to get out!

"Sunshine! Get out of there!" I cried again frantically.

She looked at me and then at the slime, and for an instant I thought she would try to come to me.

"No, girl! Go that way!" I shouted, and pointed to the only escape route left for her.

She whined softly and dropped her tail between her legs. I could tell she was scared. I was scared, too. Then, looking at me with big, trusting eyes, she crouched to jump in my direction.

"NO, SUNSHINE! THAT WAY!" I screamed.

My cry came too late. An instant later she was in the air, making a gigantic leap straight toward Luke and me across the river of slime.

My heart stopped. I closed my eyes, praying that she wouldn't land in the middle of the sea of slime.

But she stretched her long body into a golden arch and landed beside me a couple of seconds later. "Good girl!" I shouted.

I started to pet her, but the slime had reversed its direction. In a split second it had heaved itself upward and was coming after us. It was bigger and stronger than before. And since it was smaller than the main slime that had terrorized the golf course, it could move a lot faster.

"The cafeteria!" I shouted, racing out the media-room door.

I knew we only had one chance. If we could all three squeeze out through the boarded-up window and nail it shut again, the slime would be trapped inside—at least for a while.

Chapter

19

We dashed down the hall, with Sunshine out in front. I was next, and Luke brought up the rear. The slime slurped and squished after us.

"It's gaining on us!" Luke cried, throwing a frightened look over his shoulder.

My heart dropped into my stomach. *Any minute now it's going to be all around me,* I thought.

I pushed my legs as hard as I could, taking long strides and ignoring the pain in my chest. Then I crashed around a corner. My legs felt like blocks of lead, and my heart was about to explode.

Sunshine seemed to know where we were going because she rounded the last corner in the hall and burst through the swinging doors into the lunchroom. I skidded in after her and ricochetted off half a dozen tables as I stumbled wildly toward the kitchen and the broken window. I had to get more boards off or all three of us would be doomed! We'd be gulped down into an endless pool of sticky, smothering slime!

I pounded on the wood with my hands, but it held fast. Next I heaved with all my weight, pushing my shoulder against the boards. The wood groaned and budged a little, but it didn't give.

Luke barged through the door, stumbling and catching himself on a table.

"Hurry," he pleaded. "It's—it's—"

Before he could finish, the door burst open a third time and a tidal wave of green chunks rolled into the room.

I scrambled onto the countertop, pulling Luke up with me. Sunshine took one gigantic leap and stood beside us.

The slime swirled around on the floor like an angry sea, splashing sickening green waves higher and higher as it reached out for us.

This is it! I froze like a statue.

Luke was fumbling around the counter, picking up pots and pans and hurling them into the swirling slime. I looked around frantically, but there was nothing else left to do. Grabbing an iron skillet, I smashed it at the next incoming wave. It floated on top for a moment and then sank slowly into the goo.

I grabbed a pot and another skillet, hurling them into the slime. It wasn't doing any good. They were all being swallowed up. We were done for!

Chapter

I squeezed my eyes shut and waited to feel the warm slime gushing over my ankles. It was making an excited gurgling sound, as if it thought we smelled delicious. Sunshine was running in terrified little circles, barking as loudly as she could. I thought of what my dad had said over the loudspeaker on the police car. He had only wanted to help. Why hadn't I gone to him when there was a chance?

The gurgling noise had stopped, so I opened my eyes and looked down. The slime was still spread out below the counter where we stood, but it had simmered down. It was tilting slightly toward the window, listening. And in the distance I could hear the low, menacing roll of thunder that Luke and I had heard outside the golf course.

There was no mistaking it. The monster slime was rolling into Snodgrass. The slime at our feet probably wanted to join up with the killer slime outside.

Luke was still standing next to me. He had clapped his hands to his eyes to cover them, but as I watched he hesitantly lowered them and looked up.

The indoor slime had by now completely forgotten us. It slithered toward the window and reached up a few glowing tentacles.

"It's trying to climb the wall," Luke said. "It wants to get out the window."

"Quick!" I shouted. "The slime's gonna flood Snodgrass. We have to get out of town!"

Luke and I jumped down off the counter and Sunshine followed us.

We ran once more through the deserted hallways, this time toward the front door. As I threw it open the roar outside suddenly filled my ears. Out of the corner of my eye I watched the army of slime advancing across the playing fields on the side of the school.

"We'll never make it." Luke panted heavily behind me.

"Just keep running," I ordered. "And whatever you do, don't look back."

Sunshine had passed us and was running up a hill on the far side of the school—the hill that led to the parking lot.

Behind us the slime was speeding up. The low roar was getting louder. Could it have spotted us?

A stiff breeze rustled through the branches of the trees that surrounded the school grounds. And with it came an unbearable stench—like dirty gym socks and dead squirrel combined. Luke stumbled over a loose rock in our path and cried out. "We're downwind of it. Oh, what's the point?"

Suddenly he stopped in his tracks and grabbed my arm.

Sunshine disappeared over the hill. "We can't outrun it," Luke shouted wildly. "And even if we did, I just can't take this smell a minute longer." His face was as green as the slime and he clutched his stomach.

"Don't give up," I urged, pulling him along by the arm. But in my heart I knew he was right. There was no way we would outrun the slime. We wouldn't even last through much more of the stink.

Chapter

21

Sunshine was barking excitedly in the distance. *Go, girl, save yourself,* I thought. But she was running in circles as if she'd found a bone or something. A moment later I could see why she'd been barking.

The long hood of a dark blue station wagon edged into view at the top of the hill. Luke had seen it, too. "Your dad," he said. With a new burst of energy we ran toward the car. In a few seconds we had reached it. Dad had the back doors open and we jumped inside. Sunshine was already inside. Without a word he jerked the car into gear and we shot out of the parking lot.

Once out on the main road we could see that the whole town of Snodgrass was in a state of chaos. The slime stretched from the school playing fields clear through downtown.

And it was rolling through the streets in mountainous waves, sucking up everything in its path. Houses! Cars! Snapping power lines like they were pieces of spaghetti! Anything that stood in its way was history! Helicopters hovered above it, their firepower helpless to stop its advance. It was coming in our direction.

People who had ignored police orders and stayed behind were racing through the streets, heading away from the gooey green sea and screaming, "The slime's coming! Run for your lives!"

A little boy who was being dragged along by his mother was sobbing, "My kitty! I can't find my kitty!"

My dad was driving, but he kept looking at me through the rearview mirror. He had the same disappointed expression on his face as the time I had lied to my mother about not cleaning my room. I couldn't stand to see him looking at me that way.

"Dad," I said. "It's not my fault, I swear. All I did was sneeze. I don't know how my snot got started. I don't know why it started to grow."

"Your snot?" Dad swerved suddenly and pulled the car off the road. "You'd better tell me everything you know about this slime right now or Snodgrass, not to mention the rest of the state, will be destroyed while we're running away." He shook his head. "You say the slime is made of snot?"

Quickly I told him everything I knew— about my cold, about the medicine, about the sneezing—right on up to the moment when the slime had cornered us in the school kitchen.

We had put a few miles between us and Snodgrass, but it wouldn't be long before the slime was ready to take on the next town and the next. My dad was right—we had to stop it.

Luke, sitting next to me, began to fidget. "I don't think this is really the best place for us to chat," he began. "Maybe we could go for ice cream on another continent or something."

"You're right, Luke," Dad said. "This is no place for children. I'll drop you two off at Jeremy's grandmother's house and then I'll come back."

"I'll come with you," I said. "I want to fight the slime, too."

Dad's eyes were glowing with pride.

"Are you two crazy?" Luke argued. "The National Guard has been firing at that tidal wave of snot for hours and it hasn't even put a dent in the stuff. What do you think you can do? Pelt it with tissues?"

"That's it!" I yelled, jumping up and down in my seat. "It's a tidal wave of snot, simple snot. That's why it had to go to the golf course in the first place."

"I'm definitely not following something here," Luke said.

"Have you ever gotten a piece of snot on your hand? The only way to get rid of it is to wipe it off on something else—like the bottom of your desk."

"Yeah, and eventually it dries up and flakes off," Luke continued for me. "So what you're saying is—"

"Now I'm not following either of you," my dad interrupted.

"Dad, the snot needs water to keep growing. That's why it grew on those rainy days. That's why it broke into the golf course—to go for a dip in the ponds."

Dad was already turning the car around and heading us right back toward Snodgrass. "This is it," he said. "We're going to dry up that slime."

We headed to Snodgrass Memorial Airport, but at the airport access road we met a mob of newspaper reporters, police officers, and National Guards on their way out.

We fought our way through the crowd, desperately looking for someone who would listen to our story.

Suddenly something closed around my arm in a vise grip and stopped me dead in my tracks. I spun around and came face to face with a tall, skinny man with a big nose. His eyes were wild with panic.

"I've got one of them!" he shouted at the top of his lungs. "The boys who caused the slime! It's *Jeremy!*"

A roar went up from the crowd, and people pressed around me, trying to get a closer look. Photographers were unpacking their equipment again and their flashes blinded me momentarily.

"That's him, all right!"

"Yeah! He looks just like his picture!"

"Run, Luke!" I cried.

But it was too late. Other hands grabbed him, and before we knew what was happening, we were being lifted into the air and carried toward the slime. I could hear Sunshine frantically barking, but soon the sound was lost in the mass of people.

"Put us down!" I shouted. "We can help! We know how to destroy the slime!"

No one was listening. Instead they were yelling back and forth to each other, congratulating themselves for capturing us. Dad was trying to push through the crowd to talk to the officers who were holding us, but he kept getting pushed farther and farther back.

"Listen to me!" I shouted again. "We can destroy the slime!"

But no one was listening. The rumbling of the slime had stopped and it was watching us from across town. But everyone was too angry with us to notice.

"We got the nasty little brats," bragged the tall, skinny man. "They tried to get away, but we caught 'em!"

There were murmurs of agreement in the crowd.

"That's not fair," I began. "We've just escaped the green slime ourselves!"

"Yeah! It almost got us," Luke went on when I stopped to gulp in a breath. "But we figured out how to destroy it. If you'll just let us explain—"

The policemen slung us into the backseat of a squad car.

"Go ahead! What are you waiting for!" the officer shouted impatiently.

"I'll start at the beginning," I said, and rapidly told him the same story I had just finished telling my dad.

The officer's brows were knitting together in a gigantic frown. "Are you trying to tell us that this town is being attacked by *snot*?" he demanded.

"Yes, sir," I replied meekly. "That's all it is, and I know how to stop it."

"Liars!" shouted someone just outside who could hear us through the open window.

"Yeah, they've got to be liars!" shouted someone else. "That can't be snot!"

"They're probably monsters from outer space!"

"String 'em up!"

"Throw 'em in jail! They're wasting our time!"

"But you've got to listen!" I yelled. "The answer is salt! Just throw salt on the slime! You'll see what happens!"

Just then a chubby woman with bright red hair stuck her head in the car and shouted, "Everybody get out of here! The slime's coming this way and it's moving fast! They've grounded all the helicopters and called off the tanks. There's nothing left to do but run!"

The officer immediately forgot about us. So did the rest of the crowd. They were pushing and shoving each other, racing through the street to get away from the slime.

I stuck my head out the door and gasped. The slime was flowing down the street, making its way from building to building.

"We're dead meat, Germ! Even if salt is the answer, we don't have any!" Luke cried in a panicky voice. "And even if we did, it would take tons of it to stop that thing! *Nobody's* got that much salt!"

Suddenly a brilliant idea flashed in my mind.

"Yes, they do," I assured him. "And I know how to deliver it."

Chapter

I motioned for Luke to follow me and ran down the road toward the airport.

A cloud of dirt and debris was rising over the advancing wall of slime. It was eating the town!

Luke, my dad, and I were the only ones who knew how to stop it. With every ounce of strength I could muster, I propelled myself down the road, passing the last stragglers who were leaving Snodgrass for good.

"You think we're going to find salt here, I

assume." Luke grunted as he huffed and puffed alongside me.

"Remember how they put salt on the roads in the winter when it gets icy?"

He nodded.

"And remember how the city of Snodgrass keeps tons of the stuff in storage sheds out by the airport to load into trucks and spread around?"

Luke nodded again. Then he frowned. "What good does that do us? Nobody will listen to us. Even if we get to the salt, how are we going to get it to the slime?"

"Helicopters!" I shouted.

"Hey, wait a minute!" Luke protested, stopping in his tracks and staring at me. "Who's going to fly the helicopters?"

"My dad can fly one. You'll have to go find him while I track down the salt."

I took off running again before Luke could stop me. I knew what we had to do, and I was determined to do it!

When I finally reached the airport, I almost collapsed with relief. It was deserted, but a few helicopters were grounded there, sitting on the runway like a swarm of giant insects. And off to one side of the main hangar was the shed where the salt was stored.

I grabbed an old wheelbarrow from the shed and started to fill it with bags of salt. Then I hauled the load over to the helicopter.

Suddenly I heard a huge rumbling crash and felt the ground beneath my feet shake. I spun around and saw that behind me the slime had reached the tree-lined edge of the airport. It was bearing down hard on the trees and they were cracking under the weight. I just had to hope that the trees hadn't cut Dad and Luke off before they made it to that point in the access road.

Hurry! I thought. *Dad, Luke, hurry!*

My hands were shaking as I climbed up into a chopper and faced the instrument panel. I'd never seen so many gauges and dials in my life. And buttons and levers.

I glanced up over my head at the massive

blades and swallowed hard. All I had to do was get the engine started. It ought to be simple. But when I looked at the panel again, I knew that it wasn't.

I started flipping switches. Nothing happened.

I studied the panel some more. Some of the buttons and levers were labeled. I pushed the button marked STARTER. Nothing happened.

The pounding on the side of the helicopter nearly made me fall out of my seat. Had the slime come this far already? I wrapped my head in my hands.

"Open up! Open up!" I could hear two distant, tinny voices over the thundery blasts now coming from the slime. *Dad and Luke.*

I swung the door open and slid over. They jumped in breathlessly.

"You do know how to drive one of these, right, Mr. Wilson?" Luke was saying.

"It's been years." My father gritted his teeth. "But unless they've stopped making

126

helicopters the way they used to, I should be able to get us off the ground."

He fumbled around with some switches on the control panel for a moment, and abruptly the blades began to rotate faster and faster, making a gigantic whining sound over my head. The whine grew louder as the blades turned.

The helicopter leaned forward a little but didn't go anyplace.

"Up!" I yelled. "We have to go up!"

There was a stick on my left with a motorcycle-type grip. Dad twisted it, and the motor overhead whined even louder. Then he pulled up on it, and the helicopter started to rise.

"Hang on!" Dad shouted as we lifted into the air. We lurched forward and upward.

Chapter

"**W**ow! Look at that!" Luke shouted as we rose in the air and headed for Snodgrass. We could see the green slime, slurping its way from the city dump into town like a giant green tongue. I shook my head in amazement that one tiny ball of snot from one little sneeze could have grown into something like that.

"You know this isn't going to be enough salt, don't you?" Luke asked. His voice had a panicky sound again.

"I know," I said. "But don't worry. It'll be okay."

Dad banked the helicopter to the right and headed for the leading edge of the slime. When he got to it, he dropped lower and circled, making sure everyone on the ground noticed us.

The crowd of fleeing people looked up in panic. Not far away, a patrolling police car turned its loudspeaker skyward and blasted out, "GERM WILSON! LUKE DAMATO! WE KNOW THAT'S YOU UP THERE! LAND THAT HELICOPTER IMMEDIATELY! I REPEAT! LAND *IMMEDIATELY*!"

But Dad kept circling the front edge of the slime, waiting for the proper moment. Just then a National Guard officer came roaring up beside the police car in a jeep and jumped out, putting a radio up to his mouth.

"NOW HEAR THIS, WILSON AND DAMATO! YOU HAVE STOLEN GOVERNMENT PROPERTY! LAND THE AIRCRAFT IMMEDIATELY!"

The sound of his voice blasted out of speakers in the helicopter. It was so loud it made my ears ring.

"This is it!" I shouted. "The moment we've been waiting for! Bombs away!"

Luke and I scrambled behind the seat and began shoveling the salt furiously out the window. It flew through the air like a blizzard and covered an entire square block of slime.

At first nothing happened. Then suddenly the huge ball of slime shrank back and a cloud of smoke shot into the air.

People on the ground began cheering wildly as the slime slowly started retreating.

"We've still got a little more salt," Luke said from behind the seats.

"Dump it," I ordered.

A minute later a snowfall of salt rained down on the green goo beneath us. Again the slime ball shriveled and shrank in size. And again a smelly cloud of smoke filled the air.

Suddenly the radio crackled to life again. "ATTENTION, WILSON AND DAMATO.

THIS IS MAJOR MARK LONDON. CANCEL MY COMMAND TO LAND YOUR AIRCRAFT. WHATEVER YOU'RE DROPPING ON THE SLIME IS DES-TROYING IT! CONTINUE THE GOOD WORK. OVER AND OUT."

Luke looked at me in horror. "But—but that was the last of the salt onboard. We—we don't have anymore!"

I pulled the cockpit radio off its hook above Dad's head and pushed the talk button. "Major London, sir? This is Wilson."

"Go ahead, Wilson," he said gruffly.

"Sir, the stuff we were throwing on the slime is salt, and we don't have any more aboard. There are tons of it stored at the airport in the storage shed near the rest of the choppers. Maybe your men could help us out."

There was a moment of silence. "They'll be airborne *immediately*!" he barked. "And Wilson?" he added in a puzzled voice. "Snot? Did I hear correctly? You said the slime ball is nothing but *snot*?"

"Yes, sir," I replied. It took all my strength to keep from laughing. "That's why they call me Germ, sir."

"Oh, yes, right," fumbled the major. "Well, then . . . over and out."

It was quite a sight to see all those helicopters take to the air and bomb the slime ball with salt. There was a gigantic blast and a mushroom cloud of smoke. All that was left of it after the smoke cloud cleared was a pile of green ash that got swept away by the wind.

We were greeted like heroes when we landed the chopper. The mayor was there, and Major London, and the TV reporter, and Mom, and even Sunshine, wagging proudly. Mom had found her still in the car where we had left it out on the road.

The mayor made a speech, and the crowd applauded wildly. Then he handed the microphone to me.

"Germ Wilson, since you are the one who started all this as well as the one who figured out how to save the town of Snodgrass and all its people, I'm sure we'd all like to hear you say a few words."

I took the microphone and looked at the mayor. Then I looked at the crowd. And at my parents in the front row. Everyone was smiling. Even Luke was grinning beside me.

I hated to say what I was going to say, but I didn't have any choice. I sighed deeply and spoke directly into the mike.

"I think I'm going to sneeze."

About the Author

Betsy Haynes has written over fifty books for children, including *The Great Mom Swap,* the bestselling The Fabulous Five series, and the Taffy Sinclair books. *Taffy Goes to Hollywood* received the Phantom's Choice Award for Best Juvenile Series Book of 1990.

When she isn't writing Betsy loves to travel, and she and her husband, Jim, spend as much time as possible aboard their boat, *Nut & Honey.* Betsy and her husband live on Marco Island, Florida, and have two grown children, two dogs, and a black cat with extra toes.

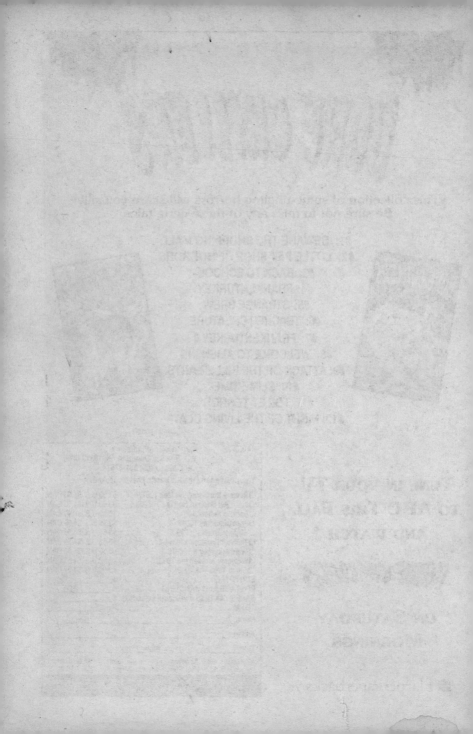